Stick-With-Me™ Bible Stories

Let's Catch Fish

John 21:1-14

by
Dr. Mary Manz Simon

illustrated by
Ron Kauffman

Carson-Dellosa Christian Publishing
Greensboro, North Carolina

Contents

Credits
Author: Dr. Mary Manz Simon
Project Director: Sherrill B. Flora
Editor: Carol Layton
Illustrator: Ron Kauffman
Creative Director: Annette Hollister-Papp
Layout Design: Mark Conrad

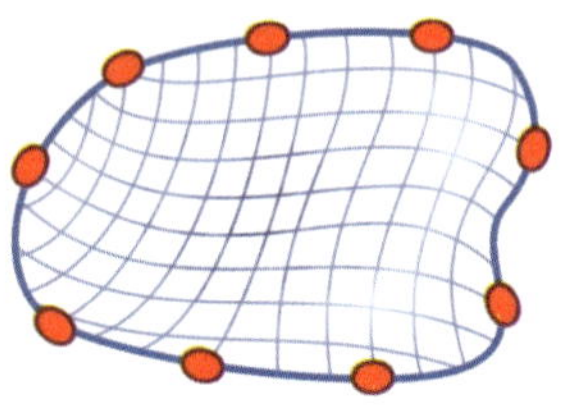

Scripture on back cover is quoted from the *International Children's Bible®*, *New Century Version®*, copyright © 1986, 1988, 1999 by Tommy Nelson™, a division of Thomas Nelson, Inc. Nashville, Tennessee 37214. Used by permission.

ISBN 0-88724-756-3

"Let's catch 🐟 **fish**," said Peter.

"The 〰️ **water** is calm,

the ⭐ **stars** shine so bright.

Let's go catch some 🐟 **fish**

by the bright 🌕 **moon**'s light."

Peter and his friends got into the **boat**.

They dropped their **net** and waited.

"Let's pull up the **net**," said Peter.

4

They pulled the 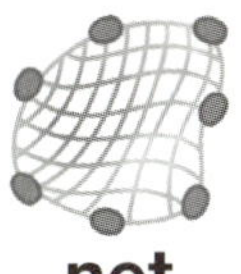 out of the  .

net **water**

"Oh no," said Peter. "No  !

fish

There are no  in the 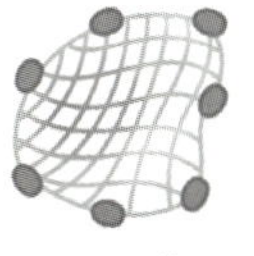 ."

fish **net**

They dropped the 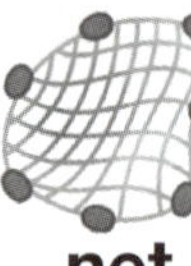 into the  again.
net **water**

Peter said softly, "Let's catch  .
fish

The  is calm,
water

the  shine so bright.
stars

Let's go catch some fish

by the bright  's light."
moon

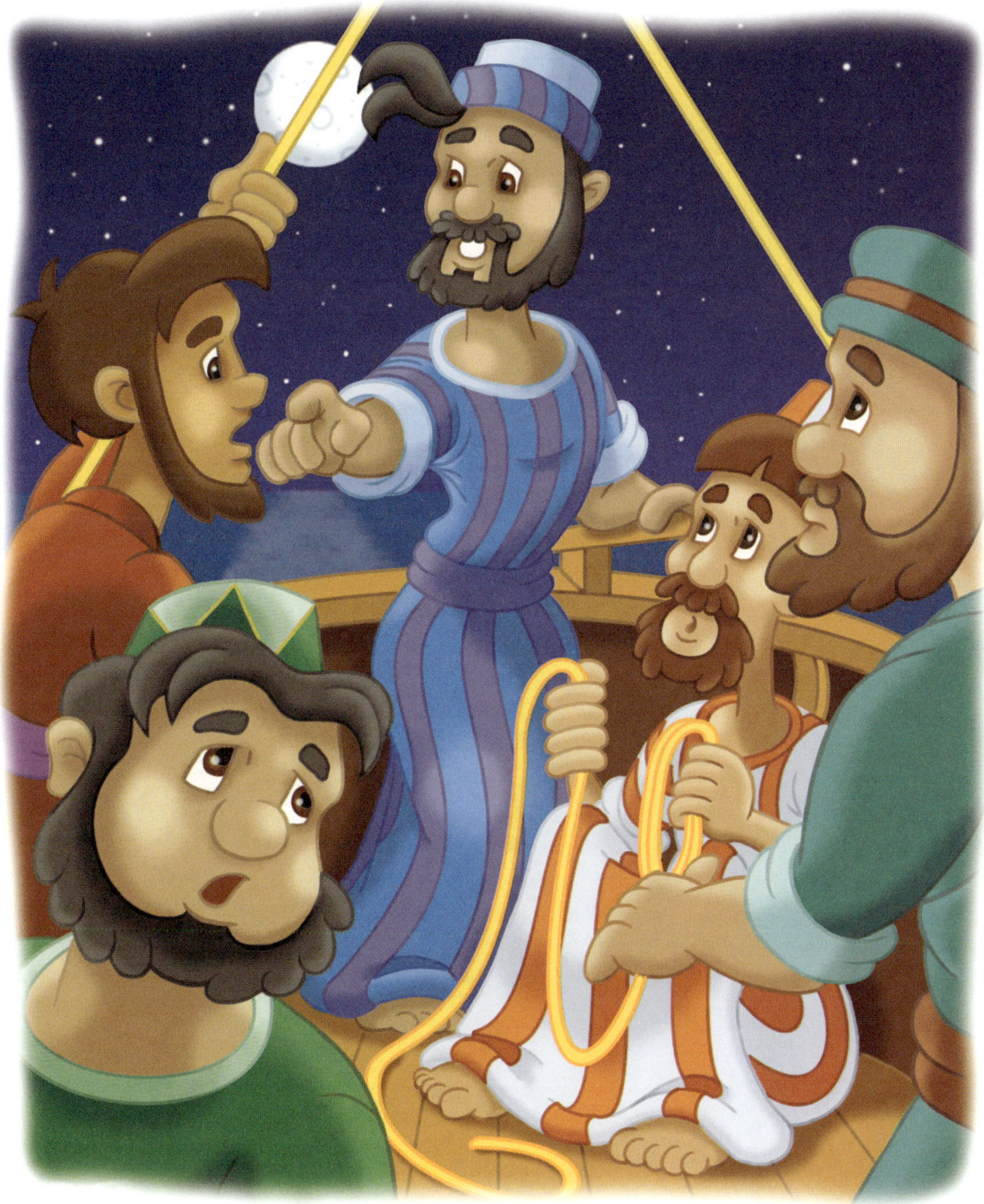

The men waited.

"Let's pull up the net," said Peter.

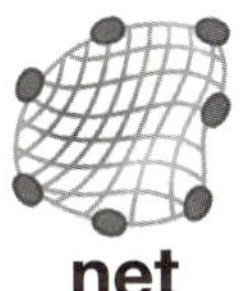

They pulled the 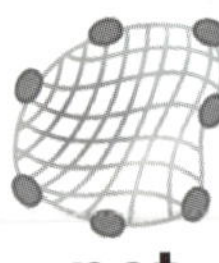 out of the  .

net water

"Oh no," said Peter. "No  !

fish

There are no  in the 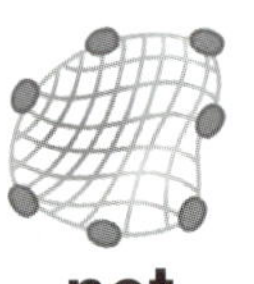 ."

fish net

Use these stickers
on page 16.
Use this
Scripture
sticker on
inside back
cover.
John 21:1-14

"Let's go home," said Peter.

The men pulled the 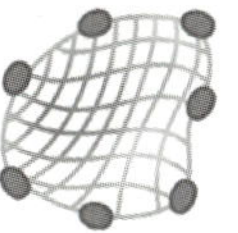 out of the 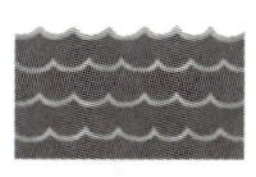 .
net **water**

A man called, "Drop your 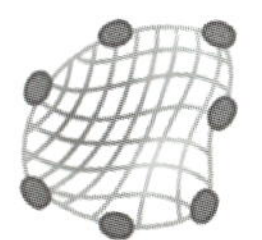 on the
net

other side of the 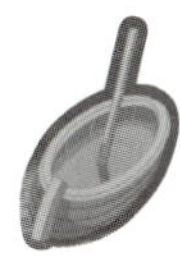 . You'll catch  ."
boat **fish**

The men dropped the 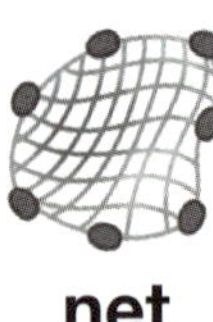 into the 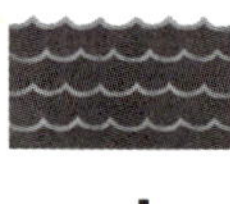 again. They waited.

net

water

Jesus had started the fire for breakfast.

Jesus said, "Bring some  ."

fish

Peter went back to the  .

boat

He dragged the full of .

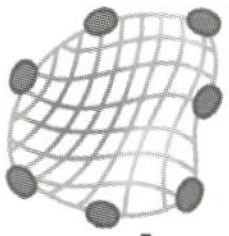

net   fish

Peter said,

"The  was calm,
water

the  shone so bright.
stars

The Lord helped us 
fish

by the bright  's light."
moon

Let's Talk

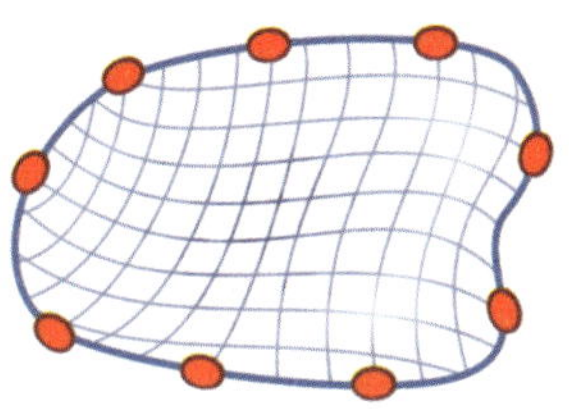

The men in the story caught fish in big nets. What else could people use to catch fish?

Who cooked breakfast for the men in the story? Who made your breakfast today?

Jesus took care of his friends by giving them food. How does Jesus take care of you?

Something's Fishy

Does a 🐟 have scales or skin?

fish

Do 🐟 wiggle or giggle?

fish

Does a 🐟 dive or live in a hive?

fish

Does a 🐟 wish or swish?

fish

Is a 🐟 wet or dry?

fish

Do 🐟 go to school or live in a school?

fish

How many types of fish can you name? ———————

1.

    dog   **fish**

2.

    king   **fish**

3.

    saw   **fish**

4.

    sail   **fish**

5.

    clown   **fish**

6.
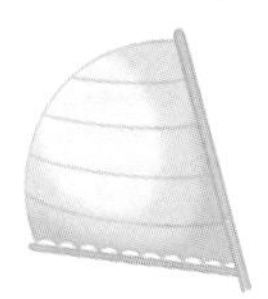

    angel   **fish**

7.

    cat   **fish**

8.

    bone   **fish**

Riddles that Rhyme with Fish! ———————

1. When my shoes are wet they:

2. My lunch is served on a:

3. A fish tail goes:

1. squish 2. dish 3. swish